Marcus Pfister

CHRIS & CROC

North-South Books
New York

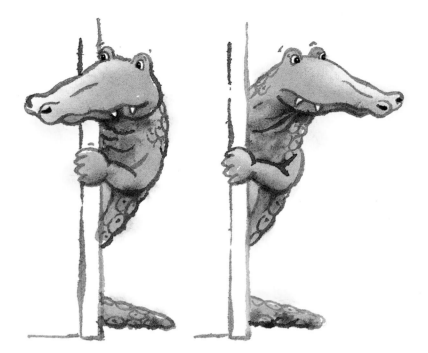

Croc was having a wonderful morning until he heard Chris yell, "Come on, you lazy stuffed animal. Let's go out and find something to do!"

Croc tried to hide, but it was no use. Chris grabbed him by his big green tail and pulled him out of the door.

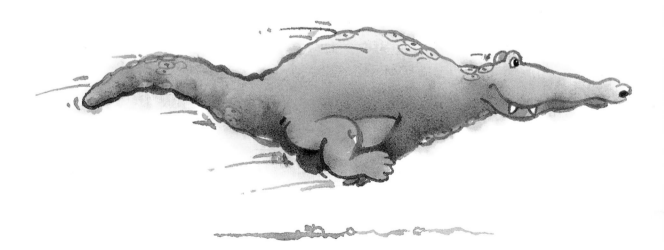

"So," said Croc as they sat on the lawn. "You dragged me out here. What are we going to do?"

"I'll come up with something," Chris sighed.

Croc got up and started to walk back and forth. Suddenly he spotted something hidden under some bushes. "Your roller skates," he yelled. "They must have been here for ages."

"Great!" Chris exclaimed, strapping the skates to his shoes. "I wonder how they ended up in the bushes?"

Chris started to roll away, but he didn't get very far. He teetered and tottered back and forth and landed with a thump on the ground.

"You're not doing too well, my boy," yawned Croc.

"Let's see *you* try it," said Chris, struggling to get back up on his feet. "Ouch, now I've hurt my knee."

Chris yanked off his skates and threw them back in the bushes. "I *hate* roller skating," he whined. "I never want to see those things again."

"Well," Croc grinned. "Now we know how those skates ended up in the bushes in the first place."

Chris and Croc walked over to a couple of boxes and sat down to think about what to do next.

"I have an idea," Croc whispered in Chris's ear.

Chris jumped up, ran into the house, and came back with some white pillows and a few belts. Croc got up and used a belt to strap a pillow to Chris's back.

"Okay," Croc said. "Now let's put one on your chest and one on each knee, and then I'll find a good stick." When they were finished, Chris looked like a real ice hockey player.

Chris skated back and forth and pretended he was defending a hockey goal. When he fell, the pillows cushioned his fall.

"I don't think your mother is going to be happy to see those pillows," warned Croc.

"It's not so bad," Chris replied as he skated towards the house. "I'll just turn the pillowcases inside out so that the clean side shows. Maybe she won't notice."

Chris came back outside carrying
his new beach ball.

"Catch," he said, kicking it to Croc.

Croc caught the ball gently in his
large mouth and ran off into the
bushes.

"Come back, you monster," yelled
Chris.

"I know you're in there somewhere," shouted Chris, creeping through the bushes. "I'll find you!" Suddenly he spotted Croc up in a tree. Chris crept up behind him and screamed, "Gotcha!" Then there was a loud pop as the beach ball burst in Croc's mouth.

"I'm sorry," said Croc, hiding the ruined beach ball behind his back. "You shouldn't have surprised me like that!"

"There goes my beautiful new beach ball," Chris moaned.

"Don't be angry with me," said Croc with tears in his eyes. "You know I didn't mean to do it."

Chris and Croc sat together quietly until Croc had another great idea.

"Parachutes!" shouted Croc. "We'll need a belt, a pair of scissors, and some string."

Chris ran into the house to get what they needed and they immediately set to work.

"First I'll cut the beach ball in half," said Croc. "Watch carefully, and you'll see how to make a parachute."

"Yippee!" cried Chris. "Which one of us gets to try the parachute first?"

"I'll go first," said Croc. "It was my idea, and I don't want you to get hurt if it doesn't work."

Croc climbed up into a tree and inched his way out on a big branch. "Here I go," he yelled, leaping into the air. "Whoopeee!"

Everything was fine until he hit the ground with a loud thump.

"Now it's your turn," Croc said as he got back up on his feet. Chris was feeling a little nervous. "Maybe this isn't such a good idea," he thought as he climbed up the tree.

Chris hesitated when he got to the first branch, but he kept on climbing. "Okay," yelled Croc. "Let's see you jump."

Chris was frightened. He was afraid that he would get hurt. But he didn't want to seem like a coward by not jumping. Then he had an idea. He decided to trick Croc.

"Hey, Croc," he cried, "look over there! Do you see that hot-air balloon?" As soon as Croc looked away, Chris crawled back down from the tree, crouched on the ground, and covered himself with the parachute.

"Wow," shouted Chris. "That was cool."

Croc turned around in surprise. "I missed your jump," he said. "Did you really sail down?"

"Like an eagle," Chris boasted.

"But I didn't see a hot-air balloon," said Croc.

"It must have floated away," said Chris with a big smile on his face.

Soon it was time for dinner. Chris and Croc went inside
and sat down to eat.

"Yuck!" Chris groaned. "Spinach!"

"Yum!" said Croc. "There's nothing I like better than lovely
green spinach. Here—feed it to me."

Chris lost no time spooning the green gunk into Croc's
gaping mouth.

"Thanks, Croc," said Chris. "It's great to have a friend
like you."